My Very First Winnie the Pooh™

Pooh Helps Out

Kathleen W. Zoehfeld Illustrated by Robbin Cuddy

SCHOLASTIC INC.

New York Toronto London Auckland Sydney
Mexico City New Delhi Hong Kong

ISBN 0-439-19897-6

Copyright © 1999 by Disney Enterprises, Inc.
All rights reserved.
Published by Scholastic Inc., 555 Broadway, New York, NY 10012,
by arrangement with Disney Press, an imprint of Buena Vista Books, Inc.
SCHOLASTIC and associated logos are trademarks and/or
registered trademarks of Scholastic Inc.

12 11 10 9 8 7 6 5 4 3   0 1 2 3 4 5/0

Printed in the U.S.A.   24

First Scholastic printing, September 2000

Based on the Pooh Stories by A. A. Milne (copyright The Pooh Properties Trust).

Disney's

My Very First Winnie the Pooh

Pooh Helps Out

Winnie the Pooh sat on the edge of his bed and looked all around his cozy house. "Nothing to do," he thought.

Pooh tried humming a little hum. "Hum de dum," he hummed. "Well, that's a nothing little hum," he sighed.

After a while, nothing to do began to feel quite bothersome.

"Maybe I should find someone to do nothing with," he thought. "That would be so much more cheerful."

Pooh knocked at Piglet's door. "Piglet," he said, "I've come to see if you'd like to do nothing with me."

"Oh, I'd like to do nothing," said Piglet, "but first I have to wash my dishes."

Pooh brightened. "Oh, may I help?"

"Yes, indeed!" cried Piglet. He handed Pooh a towel. Piglet washed and Pooh dried.

When all the dishes were stacked neat and clean in their cupboard, Piglet said, "Thank you, Pooh. That was the perfect chore for two. Now I'm ready to do nothing."

Pooh hummed. Piglet wiggled his ears and tapped his foot.

Pooh yawned. Then Piglet had to yawn, too.

"Pooh?" Piglet asked. "Are you having a lot of fun?"

"No," said Pooh thoughtfully, "doing nothing is not a LOT of fun."

"I was thinking," said Piglet, "maybe somebody needs us to help them with something."

"Something would be much better than nothing," agreed Pooh.

"Let's ask Owl," said Piglet. And with that, Pooh and Piglet set off for Owl's tree house.

"Owl!" called Pooh. "Do you need us to help you?"

"Most certainly!" declared Owl. "This dusting will get done more quickly with the help of two good friends."

Pooh and Piglet loved Owl's feather dusters—they were great for tickling and cleaning.

"Thank you," said Owl, when his home was shiny and clean. "Now I'm free to do nothing."

So Owl looked out of his window. Pooh counted up his paws, but that didn't take long. Piglet shifted in his seat.

"Maybe Tigger needs our help with something," suggested Piglet.

"Tigger!" called Pooh. "Do you need us to help you?"

"You're just the guys I wanted to see!" cried Tigger. "Picking up my toys would be much easier with three friends to help."

Piglet put away the toys on the lowest shelf. Pooh and Owl put away the toys on the middle shelves. Tigger bounced up high to put away the toys on the top shelf.

"We're a great team!" cried Tigger. "Let's go see if Eeyore needs anything picked up."

"Eyore!" called Pooh.

"Oh!" everyone gasped. Eeyore's house had fallen down.

"It's much better as a house when it's upright," said Eeyore.

"What happened?" asked Pooh.

"Just what usually happens," said Eeyore. "Wind blew it down."

"Well," said Pooh, "it looks as if you could use some help."

So Pooh, Piglet, Owl, and Tigger helped Eeyore put his house together again. Then Owl showed the others how to tie it up with string—to make it stronger against the wind.

"The best way to build a house is with friends who help," said Eeyore. "Thank you!"

"You're welcome," said Pooh. "And now I think it's time for a little something, don't you?"

"But, Pooh, we've been doing 'something' all morning," said Piglet.

Pooh patted his tummy. "Time for something to eat."

Tigger laughed. "Let's bounce over and see what Rabbit's got cooking!"

They found poor Rabbit slumped in his lawn chair, mopping his brow with his handkerchief.

"Rabbit," asked Pooh, "do you have anything good to eat?"

"I've got a whole garden full of vegetables," sighed Rabbit. "But I've been pulling weeds all day, and I'm too tired to pick them."

"May we help?" asked Pooh.

"Did you say 'help'?" asked Rabbit, cheering right up. "Why, yes, that's exactly what I need!"

"Just let me get everything organized," said Rabbit, who suddenly felt quite important and hardly tired at all.

"Pooh, you can pick potatoes, and Piglet, tomatoes. Tigger, you can pick the carrots, if Eeyore will pick the beans. And, Owl, if you would put all the vegetables in the wheelbarrow and bring them to me, I will wash them."

Soon big, juicy tomatoes, crunchy carrots, and snappy beans filled Rabbit's kitchen counter. Warm, steamy potatoes were cooking in a big pot.

"You have all been so helpful!" cried Rabbit. "To thank you, I want everyone to stay for supper!"

"Mmmmm, yummy," said Pooh.

While Rabbit finished cooking his vegetable stew, his friends all helped set the table.

"This is the best supper ever," said Pooh.

"A thank-you supper for the best helpers in the Hundred-Acre Wood!" cried Rabbit.

After the meal was over, Pooh and Piglet sat in their Thoughtful Spot for a while and did . . . well . . . they did nothing at all!

"Whew! It feels good to rest," sighed Pooh.

"Yes," agreed Piglet. "Doing nothing is much more fun after a busy day of helping."